'There should be th[...]

And there were. [...] shape. The others w[...] a bit of a struggle – [...] just about managed not to put my foot through the ceiling – I got the different bits down the ladder, into her spare room and onto the old lumpy bed there. Phew! The boxes were covered in dust, so Beryl got a cloth.

'It must be forty years,' she said, giving the things a wipe. 'I remember my Henry putting them up there.'

'I didn't know Mr Brick played the drums.'

'Well, he didn't.'

'He didn't?'

'Oh no, Charlie, my Henry had no sense of rhythm at all. These are my drums.'

'You mean you were a drummer?'

'No, Charlie.' Beryl pulled at the buckle that held the biggest box tight. 'I *am* a drummer.'

Also available by Alan Fraser from
Corgi Yearling Books:

13 PAIRS OF BLUE SUEDE SHOES

ALAN FRASER

FIDDLESTICKS

Illustrated by NIGEL BAINES

CORGI YEARLING BOOKS

FIDDLESTICKS
A CORGI YEARLING BOOK : 0 440 86606 5

Published in Great Britain by Corgi Yearling Books,
an imprint of Random House Children's Books

This edition published 2004

1 3 5 7 9 10 8 6 4 2

Papers used by Random House Children's Books are natural, recyclable
products made from wood grown in sustainable forests. The manufacturing
processes conform to the environmental regulations of the country
of origin.

Set in 14/16pt Bembo Schoolbook

Corgi Yearling Books are published by Random House Children's Books,
61–63 Uxbridge Road, London W5 5SA,
a division of The Random House Group Ltd,
in Australia by Random House Australia (Pty) Ltd,
20 Alfred Street, Milsons Point, Sydney, NSW 2061, Australia,
in New Zealand by Random House New Zealand Ltd,
18 Poland Road, Glenfield, Auckland 10, New Zealand
and in South Africa by Random House (Pty) Ltd,
Endulini, 5a Jubilee Road, Parktown 2193, South Africa

THE RANDOM HOUSE GROUP Limited Reg. No. 954009
www.kidsatrandomhouse.co.uk

A CIP catalogue record for this book is available from the British Library.

Printed and bound in Great Britain by
Cox & Wyman Ltd, Reading Berkshire.

*For all the clan
at Burnside House*

TRICKS

When Stef got the magic show, his sister Maddy went bananas. That was her gig, wasn't it? She was the stage-school princess.

'I only went along to grab a lift home,' he said, 'and somehow it just sort of happened.'

Somehow!

That's Stef all over.

Somehow he eats like four sumo wrestlers but looks like half a jockey. *Somehow* he stands up to Killer Frost and lives. *Somehow* he goes off swimming and finds he's brought along his football kit. I could go on.

'So let me get this straight,' I said. 'The thing was running late and they thought you were there to audition.'

'Exactly.'

'And you thought *why not*?'

'Well, you know.'

'So they made you climb a rope?'

'That's right.'

'For a magic audition?'

'Yep.'

'And now you're appearing in Ellington Moon's winter show?'

'Me and a few others. We're kind of sharing the job.'

'Right.'

Now, what you need to know is this – I'll keep it short – we have this theatre in Flittering. It's actually a converted chapel and most of the time it struggles along with stuff that nobody goes to. Well, nobody I know. It's things like *Mersey, Mersey – A tribute to the Liverpool Scene* or *The Teeny-Weeny Theatre Company* presents

The Anguish of Delilah. Anyway, the thing is, it's not much of a theatre, but every year, for a month before Christmas, it's *the* place to be. People come from miles and miles. Because this is when Ellington Moon takes over.

I bet you've heard of him. He's got to be the top magician around and, amazingly, he lives near Flittering. I once saw him disappear these two men who were inside a panto horse and *straightaway* they came running in from the back of the theatre.

So anyway — two weeks ago, this advertisement appeared in the local rag. It said —

Ellington Moon requires a
young assistant, aged 10-14,
for his winter show.
Auditions on Saturday
22 September at the
Flittering Leisure Centre.
Telephone 820988 for details.

Well, according to Stef, Maddy was straight on her mobile. Maddy is totally set on being famous. She's been going to this stage school for ages.

So, when what happened *somehow* happened, she went right over the edge. And just then she was upstairs having a massive stomp. She even made the ceiling shake.

'Sorry 'bout the noise,' said Stef, looking up.

'S'OK.'

'She says I've sabotaged her career.'

'Right.'

'She says I'm a hopeless amateur.'

'Ah.'

'She says I should've kept well away.'

'I see.'

'And listen – I think she's coming down.'

He was right. The banging about had turned into clumping on the stairs. The door burst open and there she was.

'I feel sorry for him,' she announced with a face like sour milk. 'When he realizes what he's done . . . I feel really sorry for him.'

Then off she slammed.

'She means Ellington Moon,' Stef explained. 'She feels sorry for Ellington Moon.'

'I know.'

And, actually, I could see her point. Sort of. I mean, with Stef, life was a bit unpredictable — a bit you-never-knew-what-was-coming. But then that was why he was such fun. Plus, we were a team — Stef Spedding and Charlie Parker.

Some people say there's a thin line between triumph and disaster, don't they? Well, Stef does the triumph and disaster. Me, I kind of feel like the line.

STICKS

Mostly, I live with my mum. It's just the two of us. She and Dad split up last year, so that's why. It was pretty awful when it happened, but it's not so bad now. I mean, it's not brilliant, but I don't let it get to me. At least I try not to.

Maybe that's why I spend so much time with Stef. There's five of them knocking around his house, so there's always something going on. And our place is a bit of a graveyard — especially when Mum's at work. She drives a van for the Co-op. And

she could drive a lorry if they asked her –
she's got an HGV licence and everything!

Anyway, the week after Stef got the
magic show, I was waiting for Mum to get
home when Beryl came round. Our house
is a semi, you see, and Beryl's the other
side. I think she's been there for ever.

'Hello, Mrs Brick,' I said.

'Oh, Charlie,' she said, 'can you help me
get something from my loft?'

'Er . . . of course. No probs.'

And it wasn't any hassle. I mean, she's a
really nice neighbour. I know she doesn't
have much money but she *always* offers me

biscuits when I pop round. And no way should she be climbing into lofts — not at her age. So I tramped next door and followed her up the stairs. When we got to the top, I pulled down the hatch and fixed up the ladder thing. Then I climbed up. I was wondering what I'd find there.

I couldn't believe it!

There was masses of junk, of course. That's lofts for you. There was even one of those dressmaker's dummy things. But the thing Beryl was after — the thing I had to get down — was a real gobsmack.

It was a drum kit!

'There should be three boxes,' said Beryl.

And there were. One was an obvious drum shape. The others were more suitcasey.

Well, after a bit of a struggle — when I just about managed not to put my foot through the ceiling — I got the different bits down the ladder, into her spare room and onto the old lumpy bed there. Phew! The boxes were covered in dust, so Beryl got a cloth.

'It must be forty years,' she said, giving the things a wipe. 'I remember my Henry putting them up there.'

'I didn't know Mr Brick played the drums.'

'Well, he didn't.'

'He didn't?'

'Oh no, Charlie. My Henry had no sense of rhythm at all. These are my drums.'

'You mean you were a drummer?'

'No, Charlie.' Beryl pulled at the buckle that held the biggest box tight. 'I *am* a drummer.'

TRICKS

It was morning break and we were looking for Spike. Everyone knew Spike was king of the back-wall smokers.

Anyway, while we were looking, I was telling Stef about Beryl and her drums.

'You wouldn't believe it!' I said. 'I mean, *we're* supposed to make the racket and *they're* supposed to have nervous breakdowns!'

'You mean the crumblies?'

'Exactly. Now we get this *clunkety clunkety clunk* coming through the wall – over and over and over.'

'I expect they're paradiddles.'

'What?'

'Paradiddles. It's a drum pattern.'

'Well, whatever she's doing, it drives me bonkers. And I can't ignore it. I mean, whenever it stops, I sit there waiting for it to start up again.'

Stef just grinned.

'You think it's dead funny don't you?'

But Stef didn't answer that. The thing was he'd spotted our target. 'Hey, Spike!' he called, running down the corridor.

Well – it was just like we thought – Spike had plenty of matches and let Stef have what he needed. Me, I couldn't believe how Stef could forget to bring his own. But that's Stef all over.

'Right,' I said once we'd found a quiet corner, 'so let's see this trick then.'

Now what you need to know is this – while I was suffering Beryl's never-ending paradoodles, or whatever they were – Stef had been to see Ellington Moon. He'd met the other assistants too. There were four of them, he said. None of the others were at our school, but one girl, Anna, lived in

Flittering and Stef said she was OK – for a girl.

Ellington Moon had this amazing room in his house – which was where they'd sat round a big table covered in a green cloth. It was like a magic museum, Stef said. The walls were covered in huge posters for old-time magicians. Against two of the walls were big glass cabinets full of fantastic stuff. There were old books and magic boxes and Chinese dragon silks and silver hoops and crystal balls and enormous playing cards and flowers made from feathers and top hats and golden wands and devils masks. Well, the way Stef described everything, it had obviously made a big impression. It did on me – and I wasn't even there.

'So what are you doing in the show?' I'd asked Stef.

'Dunno,' he'd said.

Ellington Moon wouldn't tell them. That would all come later. First they had to learn about magic. If they didn't know about magic, apparently, then they couldn't help him. Ellington Moon told them that the secret of magic was psychology. If you know how people think, you know how to fool them.

Then – to sort of prove his point – Ellington Moon taught them this trick with two matches. This was the thing that Stef was showing me.

'It's not really a trick at all,' said Stef. 'It's more sort of scientific – like an experiment. I think it's something to do with the chemicals in the match heads.'

I felt a bit disappointed at that – until I saw what he did!

'What you have to do,' he explained, 'is rub one match like this until it's charged up with static electricity.' He rubbed the thing on the arm of his sweatshirt. 'Then you balance it on the other match, like this.'

I watched. Nothing happened at first.

'Sometimes it takes a while.'

And then, amazingly, the balanced match began jumping about!

'It's the electricity,' Stef explained.

Well, whatever it was, I was dead impressed. And I was dying to have a go. 'Can I try?' I asked.

'Sure.' Stef gave me the matches.

And – just like he'd done – I rubbed and balanced and waited.

And waited.

And waited!

I wondered if I'd been set up.

'Maybe your shoes are earthing?' said Stef. 'Rubber soles are best.'

'Maybe.' I had no idea *what* he was talking about.

'Let me show you.'

And he did the whole thing again. It was so cool. Rub, balance and zap! This time, the balanced match jumped right off. 'There,' he said, 'that was a good charge.'

And that's when we heard the voice.

'What are you doing with matches?' it demanded. Loudly.

It was Killer Frost, wasn't it? Head of English and a right misery-guts.

Stef tried to explain. 'I'm just doing a tri—'

But Frosty wasn't listening. He put his face right down to Stef's. I bet his breath smelled rank. 'Matches are not allowed, boy!' he snarled.

I tried to explain. 'Yes but—'

Killer turned his head and gave me the famous yellow glare. 'Where matches are concerned, Charlie Parker, there are no *Yes buts*.'

'Yes but—' said Stef. And I know he said it deliberately.

'GIVE ME THE BOX, BOY!' Killer bellowed back.

'But I haven't got a box,' said Stef, dead calm.

Frosty hated it when his victims were calm. 'Do you want to empty your pockets in Mrs Gregory's office?' he sneered.

'Can if you like,' said Stef, still dead calm.

Well, that had Killer rattled.

'It's true,' I said, 'there isn't a box. It's just—'

'Detention on Monday,' he said, grabbing the matches. 'Both of you!'

And off he marched.

'Next time you have a run in with Killer,' I said, 'make sure I'm somewhere else.'

Stef just smiled and reached into his pocket. 'What?' he said. 'And have you miss all the fun?'

I couldn't believe it.

'Spike gave me the box,' he said, pulling out two more matches.

The next morning, I caught Stef at the

school gates. I had something to sort with him, didn't I?

'That match thing's been driving me bananas,' I told him.

'Has it?' he asked, all innocent.

'Yes, it flaming well has. I spent half the evening rubbing matches. And not one of them jumped a smidge. I didn't even get a twitch.'

'Ah.'

'So, what's so funny?' I asked. I mean, he was smirking by now, wasn't he?

'Well you know . . .'

'What do I know?'

'Well, actually Charlie . . . it's a trick.'

'But you said it was scientific! Like an experiment, you said!'

'I know I did,' said Stef, 'but actually, it's a trick.'

It took a while to sink in, then I asked him. I mean, I felt I had a right to know. 'So how's it done then?'

'Can't tell. Sorry.'

'What — after all that rubbing!'

'Sorry.'

'Stef!'

'The thing is, Charlie,' he explained, 'it's like a test. I'd like to, but I just can't. Ellington Moon said we should practise the trick until we could fool a friend. And we had to pretend it was science. That's the psychology bit you see.'

'Come on,' I said, 'just give me a little hint?' I tried to look dead appealing.

It didn't work. 'Sorry Charlie,' he said. 'I just can't.' And I could see he really meant it.

I was a bit disappointed, if I'm honest. But then, someone had to be his guinea pig, didn't they? And I was it. Squeak, squeak!

So I let it drop.

Except in assembly I whispered in his ear.

'I even changed my shoes and stood on a rubber mat!'

Well, there were tears in his eyes, but he didn't make a sound. He just sort of sat there, shaking.

4

STICKS

I was outside the Photo-Me booth by the Post Office when *she* turned up. Snobby Mrs Crabtree. Her huge garden backs onto our scruffy bit of lawn and she's known us for years. Mum calls her Crabface. And her daughter Celestine's in our class.

'Charlie Parker,' she said all superior, 'I don't know what you can be thinking! I never heard such a noise! I can only imagine your mother was out for the afternoon!'

'Er . . . I don't know what you mean,' I said. And I really didn't.

'I mean that appalling thump, thump, thump.'

'Thump thump, thump?'

'Yes, thump, thump, thump! And on a Sunday afternoon too.'

'On Sunday afternoon?'

'Must you repeat everything I say?'

'Sorry.' I wasn't, of course. But I *was* beginning to catch on.

'Mr Crabtree and I were in our conservatory,' she went on. 'We were taking tea with the Smileys. Well, the noise was unbearable!'

'You're talking about the drumming, aren't you?'

'Of course I'm talking about the drumming. What else would I be talking about? And why a boy like you should want to play the drums at all is beyond me. There are so many wonderful opportunities these days. Still, if you must play the drums, then your mother should at least ensure that you take lessons from a qualified teacher and practise somewhere appropriate. Goodness knows what Mrs Brick must think. The poor woman must be at her wits' end.'

I thought it was time to put the old bat straight. 'But it's her who's playing.'

'What do you mean, *it's her*?'

'I mean, it's Mrs Brick who's the drummer.'

'Charlie Parker! Do you think this is some kind of joke?'

'No,' I said, 'what I'm saying is that Mrs Brick has got a drum kit and she's the one you heard playing!'

I might as well have told the crack in the pavement.

'I know it's been hard for you,' she said, dead patronizing, 'what with your parents and their problems, but expecting me to swallow a story like that is frankly absurd. However . . .'

'But . . .'

'Please don't interrupt me, Charlie,' she snapped. And she put her hand to her mouth, gave a little cough and went on with her lecture. 'However . . . in view of your family difficulties and my long friendship with your mother, I shall say no more about the incident. But, in future, I expect you to find somewhere else to practise your . . . drumming.'

She made the word sound like a skin disease. Then she just stood there – like she was waiting for some sort of answer.

But I kept my mouth zipped. Well, I wasn't about to interrupt, was I?

'Well?' she said, eventually.

'Fine,' I said with a sweet little smile.

'Good,' she said.

'Right,' I said.

'I'll be on my way,' she said.

'OK,' I said.

And off she went – which left me standing there alone. For half a second.

Stef pulled back the little curtain and stepped out of the booth. 'Nice one, Charlie,' he said with a big grin.

Well, I thought so.

And that's when the photos appeared.

'Right,' I said. 'Let's make a move. Or we'll be too late.'

We were going to see my dad. He'd said that if we came to his work after five we could mess about with his new bit of kit. My dad works in computing, you see. His company develops new software. And this latest thing sounded *so* wicked – if you scanned in your photo, the screen would age you and show you how you'd look in ten or twenty years!

We got there just before six. And we had the funniest time! I can't remember when I've laughed so much! And it was dead cool the way the computer changed our noses and grew our chins and added lines and stuff. The bad news was I wouldn't be turning into David Beckham. But at least I wouldn't look like Yoda from Star Wars. The truth is, I think I'm going to turn into my dad. Well, it could have been worse. I could have been Stef! 'Cos we really messed around with his face! But he just loved it.

'What if I go bald?' he said. 'My uncle's gone bald.'

'Well,' said Dad, tracing round the hair-line, 'let's see.'

'It's Killer Frost!' I said. 'You're going to be Killer Frost!'

'I am not! It's nothing like him!'

'Yes it is! Well, all right, it's not really . . . but the hair is.' And it was, too.

Stef did his impression. 'Silence, boy!'

'Of course, you're bound to fill out in the face,' said Dad looking at the image.

'Especially the way he eats,' I added.

'Make me fat,' said Stef.

So Dad made him *really* fat.

Well, I was laughing so hard I could hardly breathe. Eventually, I managed to get a grip. It wasn't easy. It was such a hoot. He was fat, bald and forty. 'You have got to print that one off,' I said. 'You've got to take that home!'

And that's what Stef did. I took one too. But mine was much more boring. It was just me at twenty. I wanted to show Mum.

Trouble was, when I got home, Mum was having a glum-fest. I mean, she did look at my piccie and she did smile – sort of – but she didn't want to hear anything about Dad.

'Sorry Charlie,' she said, 'I've had a lousy day. The cold store at the depot packed up. I've spent the whole day salvaging fish fingers. And when I got home, the last thing I needed was Ringo Starr next door.'

'Ringo Starr?'

'I mean Mrs Brick and her nuclear drumming.'

'Right. She was practising, was she?'

'Wasn't she just! And the awful thing was, well . . . I let it get to me.'

'What do you mean?'

'I banged on the wall.'

'No!'

'I did. I mean, I should have put up with it, or gone round and talked to her politely. But what did I do? I turned into Mrs Angry and banged on the wall. I don't know what she must be thinking.'

'She won't mind.'

'I know, Charlie. But right now I feel terrible. I should go and apologize, but I just haven't got the energy.'

'D'you want a cup of tea?'

'No, it's all right. C'mon, let's get something to eat, shall we? What d'you fancy?'

'Have we got fish fingers?' I asked.

Mum smiled at that.

5

TRICKS

It was Sunday morning and I went round to see Stef. There was stuff I wanted to hear. The day before, he'd been back to see Ellington Moon.

When I got there, he was playing Snap with his little sister.

'Sorry, Katie,' he said. 'I have to talk to Charlie now.'

Well, she gave me a right look – like I'd ruined her day or something. Then she got up and toddled off.

Stef gathered up the cards. 'So how's the mad drummer?' he asked.

I told him straight. 'You don't want to know! Anyway,' I went on, 'never mind Beryl. What about you and Ellington Moon?'

'It was dead scary actually.

We all got there . . . and we went into his magic room, same as before, and everything was fine and friendly . . . for a while . . . and then he asked us about the match trick. But it wasn't anything casual. He grilled us one at a time. *So what about you, Stef? How did you get on? And did you keep the secret?* And all the time I was telling him he was looking right into my eyes. It was worse than Killer, I can tell you. Anna said it really spooked her. And when he'd finished, he said that if any of us had any doubts, then this was the time to speak up – because the next time we got together, we'd be rehearsing for the show. Well, none of us said a word. I mean, can you imagine backing out now?'

'No way.'

'So next Thursday, we're all meeting at the leisure centre. He wouldn't tell us why.'

'It's got to have something to do with

the rope climbing, hasn't it?'

'That's what we all think. But we don't know for sure. It's like he wants to keep us guessing. I think he kind of enjoys it.'

'Like with the matches!' I reminded him.

Stef smiled. 'Well this time, you'll know I'm cheating.'

'What d'you mean *this time*?'

Stef reached behind and picked up a book. 'Ellington gave me this,' he said.

It was called *Hermann's Magic*. It looked pretty old too. I had a look inside. From the state of his photograph, old man Hermann wasn't the jolly uncle sort. He looked like his hobby was pulling legs off spiders. But he'd obviously known a thing or two. There were tricks with cards, tricks with coins, tricks with balls, tricks with thimbles, tricks with cigarettes, tricks with eggs, tricks with hats. It just went on and on – for three hundred and fifty pages!

'So,' said Stef. 'Take a card . . .'

He fanned out the pack and I took one. Squeak!

STICKS

Monday detention was a real drag. Killer had a fine time – of course – being Mr Don't-Mess-With-Me, but the rest of us settled for survival. I won't bore you with the gories. All you need to know is, I got home around five, which meant I had an hour to myself.

I thought!

I hadn't even boiled the kettle, when Beryl came round.

'Hello, dear,' she said. 'I saw you get home and I thought I'd better check.'

'Oh yes,' I said, a bit puzzled.

'You see, I was hoping to do some practice, and I rather think it might disturb you.'

'No, no, it's fine.' What was I saying!

'You see,' Beryl went on, 'the other night I was working on some snare patterns and I heard a banging. Possibly your mother was hanging a picture?'

'Er . . . I'm not sure.'

'But the point is, Charlie, you see, it rather struck me − if I could hear your mother then she might be hearing me.'

'I see.'

'So if I *am* disturbing you, you will say, won't you?'

'Of course.'

'I can't tell you what a relief that is.'

'Oh, good.'

Well, I felt like a right useless dork. I mean, I'd more or less given Beryl the big go-ahead. I'd had my chance to sort things out and I'd totally bottled it. Now she had the idea that I was next door cheering her on. So I figured − since I'd soon be going bonkers − I should at least know why.

'Mrs Brick,' I said.

'Yes dear?'

'Your drumming – why is it you've started playing again? You know – after all this time?'

'Well, I've got a gig of course!'

'A gig?' Did crumblies have gigs?

'Yes Charlie – a gig. Why don't you come next door and I'll show you?'

So I went. I mean, wouldn't you?

Beryl's sitting room is sort of faded and worn. Mum says it's homely, but it makes me want to open the window and breathe fresh air. But Beryl does have some nice old things – like her silver candlesticks and a few other bits and pieces.

But that afternoon, the thing that grabbed my attention was her drum kit. It was all set out around a little stool – the way drum kits are. And on the front of the big bass drum it said *Stratford Stompers*.

'That was our band,' said Beryl. 'We started up after the war. A lot of musicians were still in the Forces, you see. Otherwise we might never have got the chance.' She went to her sideboard and picked up what looked like a scrapbook. 'Here,' she said, 'have a look.'

Well, inside were pages of cuttings and ancient photographs. I spotted Beryl straight off. It wasn't hard – the other musicians were all men. Plus she had to be the one behind the drums, didn't she? And in every picture there she was – this young woman beaming out at the camera. *Jazz Band Success!* said one of the captions.

'So you were in a jazz band,' I said.

'That's right, Charlie. And last week I got a letter from Stanley – he was our guitarist – and he said he wanted to orga-nize a get-together gig! After all these years! I'm surprised there's any of us left, but Stanley says he's traced four!'

'So . . . that's why you're practising?'

Beryl beamed. 'Exactly.'

Well, at least we weren't suffering for nothing.

Then she picked up her drumsticks. 'Would you like to have a go, Charlie?'

Of course I did!

Well, I had a brilliant time thrashing about. I really did. It was such a lot of fun. And I bet it sounded dead loud. But when it's you who's making the noise, it's differ-ent somehow. Even so, I did wonder about Crabface. But I didn't really care – cos it's not every day you're let loose on a drum kit. And Beryl seemed happy enough. Plus she showed me a few proper things – I actually learned what a paradiddle was. It's pretty tricky too. But a rim shot isn't. She showed me that as well.

'Thanks, Mrs Brick,' I said, when it was time to stop.

'It's been my pleasure,' she said. I think she meant it.

And then I had this weird thought – what if Mum had come home early and started banging on the wall? That would have been so embarrassing. I thought I'd better tell Beryl the truth.

It was a bit awkward at first – after what I'd said earlier – but Beryl just laughed.

'Oh, fiddlesticks, Charlie! That's why I came round!'

Sorted.

And there was something else – nothing to do with drumming – it was something I'd never have noticed. Not before anyway. I saw it while I was looking at her knick-knack shelf!

And I couldn't wait to tell Stef.

TRICKS

Well, first thing on Tuesday, I told Stef what I'd seen. And that evening I told his family too. 'Cos I'd been asked round for tea.

Eating at the Speddings is a right pantomime.

For starters, there's Katie and her white food. She'll be sitting there eating rice or potatoes or plain spaghetti or something cheesy or chicken. She even likes her choccy buttons white. To be fair, I have seen her attempt yellow – like sweetcorn or omelette – but never anything green or red.

Then there's Maddy with her latest wacko diet that she'll probably have read about in some celebrity mag.

And then, of course, there's Stef and his monumental appetite. I once saw him destroy a whole family pizza – a 50cm deep-pan monster with extra bacon bits – and it wasn't even a bet! My mum says his metabolism must be a biological miracle. She also says that one day he'll wear it out. She wouldn't be surprised if it packed its bags – so to speak – and cleared off to somewhere restful like the Isle of Wight. Then Stef will turn into Mr Splodge.

Well, seeing him pile on the chips, I knew what she meant.

'Stefan!' said his mum. 'Leave some for Charlie!'

'It's all right, Mrs Spedding,' I said. 'I think I've had enough.'

'Good,' said Stef, taking the few that were left.

Maddy moved her orange and nut salad around her plate. 'So,' she said to me, 'your old neighbour's got a jug thing that looks like Stef.'

'It's a Toby jug,' I said. 'It's one of Beryl's knick-knacks.'

'Who's Toby?' asked Katie.

'He's just a face on a jug, darling,' explained her mum.

'And he looks the way Stef might,' I added. 'When he's older, I mean.'

'Poor jug!' said Maddy.

Stef ignored that. 'Remember that picture I showed you?' he asked his little sister.

'The fat man with your face?' she said.

'Well that's what the jug looks like – according to Charlie.'

'It does! Honest! It's a total spit.'

Stef looked at me. 'And you don't think she'll mind me having a look?'

'Course she won't. Beryl's really nice. Bring the picture with you.'

'OK, I will. Maybe I could come over on Thursday after rehearsals?'

After tea — and a spot of token dish-work — Stef dragged me upstairs. Then he sat on his bed and started messing with some cards. The pack had been sitting on *Hermann's Magic*. And right next to it was a screw-top jar full of something brown and disgusting.

'What is that?' I asked.

It looked like something a mad scientist would hide in his cellar. I mean, in the middle of the murky liquid, was this . . . thing!

'Oh, that,' said Stef, all matter of fact, 'that's going to be a trick.'

'Right.' Something from *Hermann*, I supposed.

Stef began shuffling the cards. 'So sit yourself down.'

I sat myself down — like a happy little guinea pig.

And, you know what? He really pulled it off! I mean, somehow he *knew* I'd cut the seven of clubs. And he hadn't even touched the cards!

'Show me again,' I said, impressed.

Stef just laughed. 'No way!'

STICKS

It was Thursday evening. So I went round to remind Beryl about Stef coming round.

'While you're here, Charlie,' she said, 'come and see what I've bought.'

I followed her into the front room.

'It's a drum pad,' she said. 'It means I can practise whenever I want and I won't be bothering you.'

'Right.' Well, that was good news.

Beryl sat behind her kit and picked up her sticks.

'Listen,' she said. And she played all these muffled rhythms.

'Brilliant!' And I meant it too.

'I think I'm getting my chops back.'

'Your chops?'

Beryl laughed. 'It's a jazz word, dear. It means technique.'

I could hear that. I mean, what she was doing sounded so cool. The sticks bounced about on her pad thing like crazy. I'm pretty sure there was some paradiddling going on. And she made it all look so easy.

Then Beryl asked the question I was waiting for. 'Would you like another go, Charlie?' She knew the answer, of course. So I sat myself down. 'But this time,' said Beryl, 'let me show you a few things.'

And that's how I got my first proper drum lesson.

'Before we start,' she said, 'this is how to hold the sticks.'

I don't know how long I sat there, trying out these exercises. But I soon realized there was a lot more to drumming than I'd imagined.

'You know, dear,' said Beryl, 'some people think the drums are easy. They think it's just banging around without having to learn about scales and chords. And of course it is fun to bang around. But then, to *play* the drums, and play well, it takes a lot of hard work. That's why a good drummer will always get a gig – any musician will tell you – because a good drummer can make a poor band sound OK. But a poor drummer will always kill a gig.'

'But what you really need,' I said, 'is a good band with a good drummer.'

Beryl smiled. 'Exactly. Then you're swinging!'

And then the doorbell rang. End of lesson. Beryl left me trying out one last exercise.

I could hear the voices quite clearly. Stef had someone with him.

'This is Anna,' I heard him say to Beryl.

'Hello,' said a girl's voice. 'I hope you don't mind me turning up like this?'

'Of course not, dear. Come on in.'

Anna was small like Stef, and she had short spiky hair and these amazing eyes. It was like they'd been made-up or something. But they hadn't.

'This is Charlie,' said Stef, introducing me.

'Hi,' I said.

'Hello, Charlie,' she said, dead relaxed.

Beryl was already fetching the jug from the shelf. 'Here it is, dear,' she said to Stef. 'Charlie's told me all about it looking like your computer picture.'

Anna put her hand across her open mouth. Well, she could see what we all could see. The face on the jug was Stef – one hundred per cent no question – but older and fatter. So I hadn't been imagining it. And just so we'd know for double sure, Stef brought out the picture.

'Wicked!' he said, comparing.

'Goodness,' said Beryl. 'That is extraordinary.'

'Is it very old?' asked Anna, meaning the jug. 'It looks like it is.'

'I think he might be nineteenth-century,' said Beryl. 'My Henry bought him when we went to Margate for our honeymoon. I wasn't too keen at first but I've grown very fond of that little jug. Now he reminds me a lot of Henry and those lovely days walking on the beach, eating fish and chips . . .'

Stef handed her the jug. 'Can I come back and take a photo?'

'Of course you can, dear.'

'Meant to bring a camera today,' he said, 'but I forgot it.'

Typical, I thought.

'I like your drums,' said Anna, pinging the cymbal.

'Me too,' agreed Stef.

'Why thank you, dears. I was just giving Charlie a few pointers.'

Stef seemed to find that funny. 'Has Charlie been drumming?' he asked.

'Oh yes, dear. Charlie's very talented.'

I'm pretty sure I turned red.

★ ★ ★

'I go to school in Staunton,' explained Anna. 'We only moved to Flittering last year.'

The three of us were next door. Mum was having a telly-veg so we sat in the kitchen doing the life history thing. It had to be done of course, and it was quite interesting, but what I really wanted to hear was all about Ellington Moon.

Eventually we got there.

'So,' I asked, 'what happened at the leisure centre? Was it something to do with climbing ropes?'

Stef looked at Anna. 'I'm not sure we can say too much, can we?'

'Course we can,' said Anna. 'Charlie's your best friend. Right?'

'Yeah.'

'Well, you can't have secrets from best friends.'

That's what I thought.

'At least I can't.' Anna went on. 'I mean, some things you have to share. And you can trust Charlie, can't you?'

Stef looked across at me. 'Yeah . . .'

'Anyway,' said Anna, 'telling Charlie isn't the world.'

So they told me.

Sorted.

STICKS

For a while, I couldn't stop thinking about what Beryl had said.

I was very talented.

Me!

And I knew she really meant it too.

Plus I'd really enjoyed it. And if felt kind of natural.

So I decided.

Well, Dad gave me the money for the drum pad and Mum bought the sticks. It only took a bit of nagging. And that way we were all happy.

Beryl was too.

'Will you come and help me choose?' I asked her.

'Of course, dear,' she said. And the very next day we caught the bus and went down to Flittering Music Shop. Mum gave me money for the bus because she didn't want Beryl spending her pension. Even so I had to insist.

Anyway, when we got inside the shop, the man with the pony-tail tried to come the big expert, didn't he?

'Most beginners start with these sticks.'

Beryl soon put him straight. 'Actually,' she said, 'I think we'd like a pair of hickory jazz threes.'

So that's what we got. And for ages they were never out of my hands. I put them down to eat, of course, and to sleep and to go to school. But that was about it. And most evenings I'd shoot round to see Beryl so I could sit behind the full kit. Plus we'd talk about the Stratford Stompers and her playing days, which was always dead interesting.

'When you get them dancing,' she liked to say, 'then you know!'

'I bet they'll dance at your reunion,' I'd tell her.

She hoped they would.

And she'd give me more exercises.

'Right, Charlie, using alternate strokes, I want you to start slow and gradually speed up – nice and even.'

That sounded easy enough.

'But,' she went on, 'as you get faster I want you to play softer.'

Well, *that* was hard.

Beryl smiled at my shambolic effort. But I didn't feel put down. Because I was learning something from someone who really knew.

'You know, dear, playing fast with soft hands is very difficult. But if you can do it well, then the drums will really sing. A lot of the reggae drummers have that.'

'Reggae drummers?' I said, a bit surprised.

Beryl smiled. 'I do have a radio you know.'

Cool.

TRICKS

Now get this . . .

I was standing by the stairwell — next to the lockers — with an egg hidden in my hand.

Read that last bit again.

I should have known better. I mean, up till then Stef and his tricks had been a lot of fun. He'd turned into the school magician and I'd stood around watching him do his stuff. In a way Stef had gone for magic like I'd gone for drumming. It was a right hoot too. Spike was his biggest fan. Stef could sucker Spike every time.

'No way!' Spike would say, or, 'Do that again!'

Stef never would, of course – except when he did this trick with a rope. Somehow Stef could tie a knot in the thing without letting go of the ends. It was such a clever bit of magic that Stef would do it over and over. And *nobody* ever figured it. Least of all Spike.

Before long, Stef knew masses of tricks. He'd obviously read *Hermann* from cover to cover. And this egg trick was straight out of the loony section, I reckoned.

Now, remember that murky brown jar in his bedroom? Well the thing floating about inside was an egg! Stef had blown it empty and was dissolving the shell in malt vinegar. I've no idea how it works, but it does. And it left him with this membrane.

'Right,' he said to me in his bedroom. 'If I scrunch it up, it looks like a bit of paper.'

He scrunched. And it did.

'Now if I bat it about, eventually, it turns back into an egg shape.'

He batted. And it did. Eventually.

'So now, my clever assistant switches the

membrane for a real egg, and abra-cadabra!'

'Hang on!' I said. 'What d'you mean by *clever assistant*?'

Stef gave me his innocent look. I knew I was in trouble.

And that's why I was standing by the stairwell with an egg hidden in my hand. I was *so* Mr Guilty too. And I was sure that Celestine Crabtree had clocked my expression.

'And so,' Stef was saying to his audience, 'I toss the ball of paper from hand to hand and little by little it becomes . . . an egg.'

'No way!' said Spike, bang on cue.

I got ready to do my bit. Like I had half a chance! Celestine was on to me, wasn't she?

'Charlie's got an egg in his hand,' she announced, dead smug.

'Have not!' I protested. Pathetic, eh?

'Oh yes you have!' Celestine made a grab to prove it.

Well, the trouble with hiding eggs in your hands is that you can't grip them that tightly. So guess what happened?

I didn't actually see the egg disappear over the edge. But I heard the result.

'AND WHAT IS GOING ON UP THERE!'

It was Killer Frost!

I suppose we could have legged it. But it was one of those moments when everything goes freeze-frame. And by the time we'd switched back on, there he was.

Well, he was red in the face of course. But that was nothing new. No, it was the bits of shell stuck to his head and the streaks of yellow running down his face that gave him that extra something. Plus he was trying to mop the mess with his handkerchief, and that only seemed to spread it about. Egg's like that, isn't it?

'IS THIS SOMEONE'S IDEA OF A JOKE?' he demanded.

Well, none of us was laughing. That would all come later.

'STEFAN SPEDDING!' he bellowed.

I wasn't having that. 'It was me, sir,' I 'fessed. 'I dropped the egg.'

We all got detention, didn't we?

STICKS

That evening I asked Beryl if I could have a thrash.

'Well, of course dear,' she said. 'But won't it disturb your mother?'

'She doesn't mind,' I said. 'She's told me to go ahead.'

So I went ahead. And I really gave the drums a thumping. I mean – whack! I bet it sounded terrible, like some third-rate metal freak-out, but I didn't care – I went for it anyway.

Finally, I shut up. I could see Beryl was glad.

'I feel like that sometimes,' she said.

'I've had a funny sort of day,' I explained. 'Sort of up and down.'

'Oh dear. What happened?'

So I told her. And when I'd finished, suddenly I felt a right dork. I mean, I'd been so caught up in my own thing, I'd not asked about hers.

'So . . .' I said. 'How's it going? I mean with the Stratford Stompers and everything?'

'Well . . .'

Beryl gave me the update. Their gig had been fixed for the second Friday in December. They'd be playing in the foyer of the Theatre Royal in Stratford East. And afterwards, there'd be a party at a grand hotel. She'd have to spend a night in London. I wondered how she'd afford that. I mean, she was a pensioner, wasn't she? And she told me once how she wanted a cat but couldn't afford to keep one. Maybe she had some savings? I hoped she did. But anyway, I could see she was dead excited.

'I've been practising my rolls all day,' she said.

'Can I hear?'

Well, they were so smooth! Beryl could see I was impressed and grinned. 'Big Sid always said – if in doubt, roll.'

'Right.' I had no idea who Big Sid was.

'Come on,' said Beryl, 'let me show you.'

And I had another lesson. We started with rolls, did a bit of pedal work, then finished with some side-drum fills and a few rim shot accents. Mostly Beryl listened. She made suggestions of course, but she said that more and more I'd learn to find my own way. So she sat looking out of the net curtains, listening.

And as I was finishing off, she turned and said, 'Oh look, there's Mrs Crabtree. I think she's just come from your house. Of course I could be wrong.'

Somehow I don't think she was.

I waited two minutes — for the coast to clear, that is — then I shot on home.

'Oh Charlie,' said Mum. 'You should have been here!'

'What happened?'

Mum filled the kettle.

'Not long after you'd started drumming, the phone rang. And it was Crabface, wasn't it? She was sorry to complain — ha ha — but she felt it was her sad duty. She'd tried to be understanding, but enough was enough. And now that you were getting her daughter into detention, her patience was stretched beyond endurance.'

'What a cheek.'

'I know, Charlie. And she was *so* patronizing! She even said it was my fault for letting you have a drum kit at home!'

'But—'

Mum smiled. 'Hang on, Charlie, let me tell you.'

I hung on.

Mum went on. 'I was half-tempted to let Crabface have it. Both barrels. But, in the end, I decided to play it super-cool. So I was very calm and very polite. But boy – I really nailed her! *Oh, we don't have a drum kit,* I explained all nice and innocent. *That's Mrs Brick next door. I understood Charlie had told you that,* I said. *I hope you didn't think he was lying to you?'*

'And what did she say?'

'She didn't say a thing. I expect she was cringing with embarrassment. I mean she'd made a proper fool of herself, hadn't she? So I just waited . . .'

'And?'

'And eventually she stammered this painful apology. *I'm so very sorry,* she said. *What must you think?* It was so satisfying! I mean, people like Crabface absolutely hate to apologize for anything. And all the time she was crawling down the phone I could hear you drumming away next door. I expect she could too!'

'Thinking it was Beryl!'

Mum smiled. 'Neat, eh?'

'But then she came round?'

'She certainly did. I thought I was going to have kittens! I mean, what if you'd walked in and said the wrong thing?'

Well, I could see that.

And I could see something else too. On the table was an amazing chocolate cake.

'Did she bring that?' I asked.

Mum smiled. 'She most certainly did. It's her I'm-so-sorry present.'

'In that case, I bet it tastes better than other chocolate cakes.'

'Well, shall we check?'

So we checked.

Twice.

'About my drumming . . .' I said, licking a sticky finger.

'Yes?'

'It was quite loud, wasn't it?'

'Like a road drill, Charlie. And I couldn't be more pleased.'

TRICKS

A few days later Stef and Anna came round with a load of flyers. They looked brilliant, too.

'We had our first run through last night,' said Stef.

'On the proper stage, he means,' said Anna.

'So how'd it go?' I asked.

And they told me.

It was all a bit cramped apparently — being the Flittering Theatre and not the London Palladium — so they had to be very disciplined. The actual equipment for their bit hadn't worked too brilliantly and there were some teething probs. For one thing they could hear the motor working!

'Ellington was a bit on edge at first, wasn't he, Stef?' said Anna.

Stef agreed he was. But he'd sorted things in the end, and he'd told them a bit about his career. Stage magic was always in and out of fashion, Ellington had said, so that's why he took over the local theatre. He wanted to have a home for his magic. It was a bit like a chef in his own restaurant – if you wanted to eat the food, then that's where it was served up.

'Well, it's definitely worked out,' said Anna. 'He's sort of made Flittering famous, hasn't he?'

We all agreed about that. Then I had another look at the flyer.

Ellington Moon
The Impossible Perfected
A hundred amazing illusions
Featuring his stunning recreation of
the legendary Indian Rope Trick

STICKS

I was telling Beryl about Ellington Moon.

'He sounds a bit like Thelonious,' she said.

'Who?'

'Thelonious Monk, dear. He was a jazz musician.'

'Right.' If it hadn't been Beryl, I'd have sworn she was making it up.

'Thelonious used to say – do things the way *you* want and let the people catch up. Even if it takes them twenty years.'

He sounded as weird as his name. 'Was he a friend of yours?' I asked.

Beryl laughed at the idea. 'Oh no, dear. Thelonious Monk was a famous American. And d'you know dear, he had a marvellous friend who played the saxophone. Guess what his name was?'

'Er . . .'

Beryl clapped her hands. 'Charlie Parker,' she said. 'Just like you!'

Cool.

'Now come on, Charlie. Let's get to work. Let me hear a nice even ten-to-ten on the ride and some crisp rim shots on the back-beat.'

So that's what I did.

'Excellent, Charlie,' said Beryl, 'Now you'se swinging!'

I loved that. Now *you'se* swinging.

Then, when the lesson was over, I asked Beryl the question that had been floating around my head – sort of waiting to get asked.

'Beryl . . .'

'Yes, dear?'

'Why did you give up drumming? I mean, you're such a good player, so why did you stop?'

'Well, things were very different when I was young. Just being a girl in a band made you a novelty. It was so hard to get accepted, even by some musicians. And when the older drummers came out of the Forces, there seemed to be less and less work to go round. But I kept gigging – for a few years – until I met my Henry. And I'm afraid Henry wasn't much of a jazz fan. He just couldn't hear it, Charlie. So, in the end, there were too many things against me. I took the easy way out, I suppose. I often regret it, but there it is.' Beryl stopped for a moment. It was like she was thinking back and remembering. 'Mind you,' she added. 'I promised myself I'd hang on to my kit – just in case – and I still kept listening.'

I looked across to her radio. 'And you still are!'

TRICKS

I didn't see much of Stef for a while. We hung around at school of course, but afterwards he always went straight to the theatre.

'I can hardly wait,' I told him one lunchtime.

The show opened in less than a week and Stef had got us freebie seats. Anna would be the one on stage. Ellington Moon had chosen her for the first night because she'd done a load of mime classes at her school. Stef said it really showed.

'You're going to be so impressed,' he said.

And I knew I would be.

STICKS

Well, what with Christmas round the corner, you can imagine, can't you? There was
one thing I really, *really* wanted.

A drum kit of my own.

The trouble, of course, was the money.

I mean, drum kits don't cost peanuts.
Even peanuts cost peanuts. And with Mum
and Dad being split and everything, I
wasn't sure how to play it. One thing I did
know was they wouldn't be getting into
some stupid spending contest. I overheard
them discussing it and they agreed that
staying out of debt was the best present
they could give me. Well, I could see the
sense of that.

But it didn't help with my kit problem, did it?

And neither did Beryl. When I asked her advice she just said, 'Goodness dear, you can always play my kit. Why don't you wait a while?'

Well, I didn't want to wait a while. So I reckoned the answer was to buy second-hand.

I talked it through with Mum and Dad and, in the end, they agreed.

'As long as you don't get carried away,' said Mum.

'Finding the right kit may take a while,' said Dad.

In other words, I'd have to be *sensible* and *patient*. But it was fair enough, I suppose. Plus Dad said he'd help with the looking around, and that sounded good to me. So we checked out the free-ads in all the local papers, and we found some sites on the Internet. The trouble was all the kits for sale were either a million miles away or massively too expensive. I began to feel that being *sensible* and *patient* was not an easy gig!

Then one Saturday morning, Dad suggested we ask the man in music shop where I'd got my sticks. So that's what we did. We went down there with a load of questions. But it was a total waste of time. He was really sniffy! I mean, he was no help at all.

Dad sussed him straight off. 'He wanted us to buy a new kit,' he said when we got outside.

If only, I thought.

And then, amazingly, as we were walking to the car, I saw this card in the newsagent's window.

FOR SALE.

DRUM KIT.
SUIT BEGINNER £50.
TEL. 640466

It had to be fate!

Dad got out his mobile. 'Let's have a look,' he said, tapping in the number.

Well, by now, my heart was racing. I mean, by the end of the day I could have my very own drums! Then, suddenly I got all panicky. What if the kit had been sold?

But it hadn't. Dad switched off his mobile. 'It's only round the corner,' he said. 'We can go and see it now.'

'Brilliant!'

Do you ever have that feeling that something is meant to be? Like you can't go wrong? Like you haven't done your homework, but somehow you're sure to be tested on the one thing you knew anyway?

Well, be warned.

The kit was complete rubbish. I mean, it had *been* a kit, but right then it was a project. I bet it would've cost loads to put right. And even then the cymbals would still sound like pan lids. It really was rubbish. But the funny thing was – for a few weird moments – I still wanted it. I suppose it was the disappointment or something. I'm so glad Dad was with me. I mean, if he hadn't been, I actually might have bought it. And the man who was selling the kit was a right geezer. He acted like the thing was the world's greatest bargain. But Dad handled him brilliantly.

'We'll have to think about it,' he told the man, as we were leaving. Then as soon as we came away he said the words I needed to hear, 'What a heap of junk!'

'It was, wasn't it?'

'*Suit Beginner*. Suit bonfire more like! Come on,' said Dad. He could see I was a bit gutted. 'Let's go for a shake.'

So we set off for one. And that's when we ran into Stef and Anna.

I introduced Anna to my dad.

'Have you been rehearsing?' Dad asked. He knew about the show.

'Oh, we've finished for the day,' said Anna. 'Stef and I are just going back to my house.' Anna looked across to me. 'Maybe Charlie would like to come along?'

'Well . . .' I said.

Dad could read my mind. 'You go with them, Charlie,' he said. 'We'll have a shake some other time.'

Dad's good like that.

'See you tomorrow,' I said.

Anna's house was a right mess. It looked like the place was having a nervous breakdown. There were stacks of books and piles of papers and half-unpacked shopping and loads of washing-up and a little army of empty bottles and bags everywhere and kicked-off boots and about fifty coats piled over the banister knob.

'It's always like this,' said Anna. 'The only time it's tidy is when we have visitors. Just before they arrive, Mum gets tidy fever. It's stupid really 'cos whoever's been invited gets the nice tidy house and we just get the bad temper. And as soon as they've gone, it's back to this.'

'Cool,' said Stef. Mess didn't bother him.

'Right,' said Anna. 'Let's have a shake.'

The shakes – two ripe bananas, two spoons of soft brown sugar, three scoops of ice cream, a slurp of vanilla, and a litre of milk, all whizzed in a whizzer – were the absolute business. We drank them in the front room, among the mad clutter. Stef got through his in double quick time. I bet he'd have massacred another one if he'd had the chance.

'All these videos,' he said, looking at the bookcase full of them.

They seemed to be the only things in the

room that weren't thrown about.

'They're for my dad's teaching,' said Anna. 'Film Studies is his main subject.'

Both Anna's parents were teachers.

She got up and went across to the line of videos. 'This is supposed to be the best film ever,' she said, pulling one out.

It was *Citizen Kane*, directed by Orson Welles.

'Orson Welles?' said Stef. 'I know that name. He used to do magic.'

'That's right,' said Anna. 'I think he did.'

Me, I'd never heard of him. And I said so.

Anna was surprised at that. 'But he's so famous!'

'Well actually,' said Stef, 'I only read about him a week ago. And I didn't know he directed films.'

'You're joking!' said Anna.

'Maybe he's a bit like Thelonious Monk,' I said.

'What!'

'You know, Orson Welles is famous *if* you're into films or magic, like Thelonious Monk is famous *if* you're into jazz.'

'Thelonious who?'

'Monk.'

'You're making it up!'

16

TRICKS

It was Tuesday night and in a few minutes, Ellington Moon would be walking onto the stage.

Me and Stef had terrible seats. They were upstairs in the back row of the side balcony. We had to turn our heads to see the stage, which was a right pain in the neck. Literally. But at least we had seats. And they were free. I bet the theatre had been sold out for weeks.

Half an hour earlier we'd met Anna outside – to wish her good luck and everything. But we hadn't been backstage.

All around us, people were talking the way they do when something special's about to happen.

'Malteser?' said Stef. He had a monster bag of them. Naturally.

I took one.

Suddenly, the lights began to fade and everything went quiet.

Then the curtains opened.

The stage was lit by this faint red and blue glow. In the middle was a tall screen thing covered in pictures of peacocks and stuff. Apart from that the stage was empty.

The whole theatre sat in silence. Frosty would have loved it. Eventually, Ellington Moon walked on from the side. Some of the audience started to clap, but before the rest of us could join in he raised his hand. 'Wait till I've earned it,' he said with a smile. A few people laughed at that, then we all settled back and waited. 'The first thing,' he went on, 'is my outfit. I've been wondering what to wear. This is my eleventh year in the theatre and I figure I should make some sort of effort. So what do you think?'

What we all thought, I'm pretty sure, was that he looked dead ordinary. He was wearing cargoes, trainers and a sloppy grey shirt. He looked OK – a bit like my dad actually – but ordinary. And definitely not Mr Showbiz.

He walked across to the screen 'Of course a lot of people expect a magician to dress like this.' He moved the screen to one side, and standing there was this shop window dummy dressed in full penguin wear. Black tails, white tie – the whole works. 'Mind you,' he said, moving the screen back, 'there is one thing missing.' He went over to the side of the stage, disappeared for a moment, then came back with a top hat. 'How's this?' he said, putting it on.

Then he amazed us. He just walked behind the screen and out the other side. And – zap – he was wearing *all* the evening stuff.

Cool.

Like his posters said — it was the impossible perfected.

'But now ... we need a little more colour.' Well, when he moved the screen again, we could see what he meant. For starters, the dummy was holding a huge bunch of red roses. Ellington Moon took one flower and put it in his buttonhole. But the real splash of colour came from the rainbow boxer shorts. The magician's street clothes were draped across the dummy's arm, and the crazy underwear was *all* it was wearing. Well, talk about Technicolour Dreampants! The magician smiled. 'These are for people who like to go a little wild in the privacy of their own trousers.'

A lot of people laughed at that. And everybody knew they were in for a fantastic evening.

It just blew you away.

By the interval we'd seen more than enough stuff to keep us talking for weeks and weeks.

'Did you notice how his flower kept changing colour?'

'And where did that aquarium come from?'

But if anything, I liked the ordinary stuff better. I mean, it's dead impressive to see buckets of paint turn into fountains of confetti, but when someone chooses a word from a book – any word from thousands – and *already* Ellington Moon's written the thing down, well, it kind of knocks you over.

In the second half he came out dressed in a loose blue shirt. Then he went into this whole series of unbelievable tricks using everyday stuff. All his props were lying on this little table at the side of the stage. One of them turned out to be the membrane of an egg! I gave Stef a big nudge at that point.

But the thing that had everyone totally gobsmacked and that lived up to all the hype – was the Indian rope trick.

'This is it,' Stef had whispered when Ellington Moon had picked up a tiny wooden box punched with holes.

'And now,' said the magician, 'I want to introduce you to a friend of mine.' He opened the lid. Inside ... was a white mouse. 'This is Anna,' he said, putting down the box. And as soon as he did, the mouse ran up his arm and walked around the back of his shoulders where it stopped to sniff the air. 'Cute eh?' said the magician. 'But what Anna really likes to do is balance on a rope.'

The rope came from his pocket. It wasn't very thick and it wasn't very long. 'Come on, Anna,' he said, collecting the mouse from his shoulder, 'time for your special exercise.' Then he stretched the rope between his hands . . . and, like it could hardly wait, the mouse scampered straight across! I don't know how it didn't fall off, but it didn't. It was like a tiny circus act. 'Coming back?' Ellington Moon asked the mouse. And bang on cue it scampered back.

'How about a little appreciation for Anna?' he asked us. And quite right too.

Well, while we were clapping our hands, Ellington Moon reached across, picked up the box and popped the mouse back in. 'And just room for this too,' he said feeding in the rope. Then he closed the lid, took a scarf from the table and covered the box. It was a very big scarf for such a small box. But there was a reason for that.

Ellington Moon held the covered box from above. He only needed a thumb and two fingers. But in a few moments, he needed both hands.

Underneath the scarf, the box began to grow. Slowly – but very obviously – it got bigger and bigger. Before long it was so big and so heavy that the magician had to drop it on the stage.

He pulled the scarf away.

The wooden box – still punched with holes – was the size of a small packing case.

Ellington Moon opened up the lid and looked down. 'Interesting,' he said. And he pulled out a rope – about five metres long and as thick as a candle. Then he coiled the rope around his arm and, while he was doing that, he had another look inside. 'Very interesting,' he said, raising his eyes. That's when he asked us, 'Shall we say hello to Anna?'

And up she popped. I knew she would of course, but it was still amazing. And you could hear people gasp.

Anna jumped out of the box and took a little bow. She was wearing a white T-shirt and white cut-off trousers — a bit like a bleached-out sailor.

'I wonder if this Anna can balance on our rope?' said Ellington Moon.

This Anna smiled. 'I think I'd rather climb it.'

'In that case, I think I'm going to need some help. Maybe we should borrow an idea from the Indian fakirs?'

Ever so quietly, Indian music started to float around in the background.

'What I mean is . . .' said Ellington Moon, 'maybe we could perform the legendary Indian rope trick?'

The music got louder.

Anna moved to the middle of the stage where she stood with her arms folded in front of the black back-drop. As soon as she got there, Ellington Moon uncoiled the rope from his arm and began shaking wavy patterns across the stage – a bit like a cowboy. Everyone could see it was just a plain ordinary rope.

And then he took one end of it and tied a knot.

The music grew even louder.

Ever so slowly, the magician looked around the theatre. He was telling the audience, *Watch this!*

We watched.

And what we saw was Ellington Moon throw the knot into the air.

Where it stopped!

I mean, suddenly, about four metres of thick rope just stood there, dead straight, like it was frozen solid, like it was hanging from nowhere, like gravity had gone bananas.

I bet everyone was looking for some sort of wire. But they couldn't have seen one. And the stage lights were pretty bright too.

Then, with a big smile, Ellington Moon grabbed the rope and walked across to Anna. The rope just went with him — like it

was tied to an invisible elephant or something.

Ellington Moon looked at Anna then pointed up to the knot.

And Anna climbed up there!

She just took hold and climbed – like the rope was hanging from a gym bar.

It really was unbelievable! Not to me of course. Or Stef. I mean, we knew, didn't we? But to everyone else – well, there was just no way to explain it. No way at all.

The psychology was perfect.

And then, just as the audience was trying to take it in, there was a big flash and a cloud of red smoke.

Anna had disappeared. And the rope was falling loose upon the stage.

Wow!

I mean WOW!

STICKS

At school, Stef had become the big celebrity. It was two weeks into Ellington Moon's show, and Stef had been on stage three times. Maddy hated all the attention he got — of course — but Stef wasn't bothered. And everyone who'd seen him climb the rope was so impressed. Spike for one.

'It was just brilliant,' he kept telling everyone.

I bet it was too. Me, I hadn't actually seen Stef do his stuff. But I would soon. Dad had bought the tickets. And Anna was coming with us.

'Now you will be on stage that night?' I asked Stef. We were walking home from school at the time. And with Stef you have to keep checking these things.

But he didn't seem to hear me. He was staring at the window of this gloomy little shop called Flittering Antiques.

'Look,' he said.

'What?'

Stef pointed. 'There.'

And I saw it. Because sitting among the bits of silver and blue patterned bowls was a jug with Stef's face. A fat and forty Stef. Exactly the same as Beryl's. And hanging from the handle was a little label.

C19
Staffordshire
£150

'A hundred and fifty quid!' I said. 'That's a drum kit.'

'Or a Chinese Guillotine,' said Stef.

I assumed that was some kind of magic trick.

And it meant that Beryl had a valuable antique. I couldn't wait to tell her.

As soon as I'd dumped my school stuff, I shot on round.

Beryl opened the door wearing this house-coat thing.

'Oh hello, Charlie, did you want a lesson? I'm afraid I've started packing my kit ready for the journey.'

'Oh no, Mrs Brick, it's not that. It's not that at all. It's about what I've seen in town. There's something I want to tell you.'

'Goodness dear. You'd better come on through.'

It was like Beryl said – the drum kit was all taken apart ready for the boxes. She'd be going off to London in the morning.

'It's your jug,' I said. 'the one with my

friend's face. I saw one just like it in Flittering Antiques and—'

And that's as far as I got. I just stopped dead. And the reason was the jug itself. I couldn't see it. I had this funny feeling too. 'Mrs Brick,' I said, 'where is your jug?'

'Well dear,' said Beryl. 'I expect it's just where you saw it — in the antiques shop.'

'You mean . . . you sold it?'

'Yes Charlie. I'm afraid I did. I got this card through the door, you see. It said *Flittering Antiques — Free Valuations*. And I thought that maybe there was something I could sell. So I telephoned the shop and the man came round. I didn't much like him to be honest. He reminded me of those spivs who cheated my mother during the War. But the truth is Charlie, I need a few extra pounds for my trip. For one thing I want to order a taxi to get to the station.'

'But Mum can give you a lift!'

Beryl smiled. 'I know Charlie. But I just want to do things properly. Just this once.'

'So . . . so you sold your jug?'

'Well dear, I didn't plan to. It just sort of happened. I was actually thinking he might buy my candlesticks. But he said they were only silver plate. And then he saw my jug. And the way he talked . . . he made it sound . . . well, it is only a possession isn't it?'

I could tell she really *really* didn't mean that. She even looked a bit misty-eyed. But then she took a deep breath.

'Oh fiddlesticks, Charlie!' she said. 'And besides, he gave me quite a bit for it — twenty pounds.'

Twenty pounds! I didn't know what to say. But I knew she'd been ripped off.

STICKS

Anna came straight from the theatre and met me and Stef for a shake. She'd just done her Saturday matinee. But, right then, we weren't talking magic at all. We were talking Toby jugs.

'Twenty pounds!' she said. 'That's such rubbish!'

'I know.'

'What a rip-off!' she added.

'I didn't dare tell Beryl what he's selling it for,' I said. 'I mean, what good would it do?'

'None,' agreed Stef. 'Best thing she never finds out.'

'So when does she get back from her gig?' asked Anna.

'Around six,' I said. 'I'll go round and see her later.'

'And d'you think she'll keep on drumming?' Stef wondered. 'Now that she's done the gig?'

'I hope so,' I said. 'It's so cool to hear her play.'

'And what about your playing?' asked Anna. 'Any news on the kit?'

Well, that was a tricky question. You see, Mum and Dad now had the brilliant idea that unless something irresistible turned up, I should wait till after Christmas. They'd obviously been discussing it. The argument was that things were always cheaper after Christmas – including second-hand.

'I suppose that makes sense,' said Anna. 'I mean, all the people who get new stuff will be wanting to unload their old gear.'

Old gear! That sounded worse than second-hand. But Anna was right, I suppose. As usual.

★ ★ ★

Beryl took a sip of her tea.

'Well dear,' she said with a big smile, 'if you want to hear the whole story . . .'

Well, I could see she was dying to tell me, so I took a sip from my mug and got myself ready. 'All of it,' I said.

And that's what I got.

It wasn't the least bit boring.

Everything about the reunion was just wonderful. She'd met friends she hadn't seen for fifty years. And not just musicians. There were people she'd grown up with – people from the East End markets and back street workshops, people she'd gone up West with to drink coffee at Lyons Corner House, people who'd shared their ration books so they could bake a proper cake, people who'd danced the Jitterbug Jive when it was the very latest craze.

The gig itself felt like they'd never stopped playing – like it was just the week before that they'd *lit a fire* beneath the dancers at the Whitechapel Co-operative Hall. Somehow, it just came flooding back. She knew the polish was gone, of course, but it still *felt* the same. Deep down.

The best thing was to see the people dancing. Nobody asked them to — it just sort of happened. And when it did Beryl felt she was seventeen again. The Stompers were swinging — and she was driving the band.

Stratford
Stompers

Afterwards, there'd been a marvellous party in the dining suite of a hotel by the river. Beryl said she spent the whole time laughing. The stories – and the wine – just kept on flowing and flowing.

And – get this – the whole thing had been recorded by the BBC! Stanley had arranged that as well! The Stratford Stompers were going to be turned into a radio programme.

'Just think, Charlie. After all these years! Me! On the radio!'

'It's brilliant,' I said. 'And will you be gigging again?'

'No dear. Not again.'

She sounded so sure of it. It surprised me. 'Why not?' I asked.

'Well, when I'd finished the gig, I realized it was over. I'd got my chops back and it felt wonderful to play again. And it made sense of all those years of storing the kit in the loft. It made sense of the promise I'd made myself. But now that it's over . . . well, it's over.'

'But what if Stanley gets another gig?'

Beryl smiled. 'Stanley's not very well, dear.'

I didn't know what to say. And Beryl could tell.

'Oh, he'll be fine for a while yet,' she said.

'So what will you do with the . . . um . . .'

'The kit, Charlie? Well, what d'you think I should do?'

It was really weird. Somehow, I kind of felt that Beryl was asking if *I* wanted her kit. It was just the way she looked at me. But then, that couldn't be true, could it? I mean, the kit was like a link to her past and everything. And she'd already lost her Henry's jug. I didn't know what to say. I just hoped the kit wouldn't disappear up the loft ladder.

'Um . . . I'm not sure,' I admitted.

Beryl burst out laughing.

I had to shift my bed to make room. And even then I could hardly open the door. But so what!

I had a drum kit.

ME!

The way I set it up meant that when I

sat on the stool I could see Celestine's house. I wondered what would happen when her mum found out. Right then, I couldn't have cared less.

It was time for a celebration thrash, wasn't it?

The funny thing was — after a few minutes — I was all drummed out. I couldn't figure it at first. I mean, I could have played for ages. I should have played for ages. But somehow I didn't want to. Then I realized — I wanted to share the way I felt. I wanted to talk about it.

Mum was surprised to see me. 'Finished already?' she said.

'I'll have a good play in the morning,' I said.

Mum smiled. 'OK.' I bet she was dead relieved too.

'So you knew about it all along?' I said, meaning Beryl's brilliant present. 'You and Dad?'

'Well, we knew that Beryl was thinking about it. She told us a while ago. But she said she'd have to play her concert before she'd really know.'

'And all that stuff about waiting till after Christmas?'

Mum touched the side of her nose. 'Aha!'

'I can hardly believe it! I've got a drum kit!'

'And you really like it?'

'I love it!'

'You're not worried that it's fifty years old? You won't be wanting a new one in a few months' time?'

''Course not.' All that would be a long way off. Besides, Beryl's kit *sounded* brilliant. That was the thing that mattered. And she'd taught me that.

Except it wasn't Beryl's kit. Not any more.

It was my kit!

TRICKS

Unless it's tipping it and Dad picks me up, I always call for Stef on school days. And I never know what I'm going to find. Sometimes he's ready, sometimes he's not. Once, when his mum had taken Katie to the doctor, he was still in bed. A lot of the time he can't find his stuff. Quite often he comes out eating toast. It's probably his fifth slice too. But it's always fun.

And that morning we were full of it.

It was the last day of school and that evening Stef was climbing the rope. And I'd be watching him do it. At last.

Well, school finished after lunch that day and we came away feeling pretty good about life.

Round the corner some Year Nines had made an ice slide.

'Watch this!' said Stef.

Somehow it didn't surprise me.

Lucky for Stef, I found Maddy and she called their dad.

'I just knew it,' she said to me, all I-told-you-so. 'I knew he'd mess things up. I knew Ellington Moon would be sorry.'

Stef spent the afternoon in Casualty.

Dad had got us balcony seats, but in the middle this time.

'D'you and Stef want some sweets?' he asked.

It was a stupid question.

And yes, Stef *was* sitting in Anna's seat! He'd managed to hobble up the stairs – just about – but no way could he leap out of boxes or climb ropes. It was lucky nothing was broken. But, even so, it meant I wouldn't be seeing him on stage at all. Typical. Instead, I'd be seeing Anna for the second time! She was his replacement.

'I feel like a right plonker,' Stef admitted.

'I'm not surprised.' He didn't deserve any sympathy.

'I don't suppose I'll be going up again.' He meant the rope of course.

'No, I don't suppose you will.' The last performance was only three days off.

It was weird seeing the show the second time round. I found myself comparing stuff and noticing things I hadn't before. But it was still fun. Dad was really knocked out. At the end of the flashy first half he'd turned to us and said, 'You know, you're never too old for magic.'

When the show was over Dad went to the pub and Stef and me went backstage. Ellington Moon was busy with his props, but he came over to say hello and Stef introduced me.

'Charlie's seen the show twice,' he said.

Ellington Moon looked impressed. 'Well done, Charlie. And did you enjoy it?'

'Oh yes,' I said.

And somehow I didn't feel an outsider at all. I even spent a bit of time telling

Ellington Moon about Stef and the egg trick. He liked that and laughed out loud.

And I liked him. He just seemed nice and ordinary. Best thing though, was when we left. I got invited to the last night party.

Cool.

STICKS

It all started in my bedroom.

We were sitting up there admiring my kit.

'It still seems unreal,' I admitted. 'I just wish I could buy back Beryl's jug as a thank-you.'

'Not at £150,' said Anna.

She was dead right. But the fact that that conman was cashing in at Beryl's expense still made me mad.

'Can I have a go?' asked Stef, picking up the sticks.

Well, I was waiting for that. The truth was, I'd have been disappointed if he hadn't asked.

''Course,' I said. I just hoped Beryl wasn't listening. She might have thought it was me! It was *painful*. Luckily Mum was working late. Anna covered her ears.

Eventually Stef got the message. 'I think I'll stick to magic,' he said.

I didn't disagree.

And that's when we got talking. We kicked off with magic, then moved on to Orson Welles, followed by Thelonious Monk, Beryl's radio show, Toby jugs, antique dealers, old books, what happened if you mixed ink with cold tea, and magic again.

And, somehow, when we'd finished, we had this mad plan. It all started out as a bit of a joke, but by the end of things Stef was getting serious.

'We can do it!' he said.

I thought he was barking. 'You are kidding?' I said, expecting Anna to agree with me.

But she didn't. She let it sit for a bit, then said, 'Maybe we could.'

'What!'

I took a bit of convincing, I can tell you. But like Stef and Anna said – all I had to do was tag along. They'd do the clever stuff.

And we could just about pull it off.

TRICKS

It was Saturday afternoon. So it had to be then or not at all. Monday was Christmas Eve, which meant we'd all be buried in the festive panic. Me, I still had my dad to sort. And bits for my mum. But all that would have to wait 'cos right then we were on our way to Flittering Antiques. You could've spotted the shop from miles off. It was the one window with no hint of Christmas. No holly, no tinsel, no Santas. Nothing.

But what it did have was a Toby jug. It was still sitting there, thank goodness.

We all went in.

Inside, the shop felt half-asleep and smelled of polish. In the corner was a big grandfather clock. It seemed to tick slower than other clocks.

The antiques man was sitting in an old armchair reading a pink paper. He had on this yellow waistcoat and a green check suit. And puffing out the top pocket was a red silk hanky. So this was the creep who'd swindled Beryl.

'Well, well,' he said looking over his little professor glasses. 'You again.'

'Hello,' said Anna, all bright and breezy. But the dealer had been talking to Stef.

Because Stef had hobbled in the day before. He'd told the dealer he wanted to buy the Toby jug in the window. The dealer had been a bit snotty, but when Stef asked how much it was the antiques man had told him. Then he'd laughed out loud. Stef, you see, offered him forty pounds. Then Stef had hobbled out looking disappointed.

Now Stef was back.

The dealer raised his eyebrows – like he was halfway surprised and halfway hopeful. 'Have you got some more money?'

Stef held up the book. ''Fraid not. But I've got this.' It was *Hermann's Magic*.

'Oh yes?' The dealer looked dead couldn't-care-less. I bet he practised in front of a mirror.

'I wondered if it's worth anything?' said Stef.

'I shouldn't think so,' said the dealer. 'Besides, books are a very specialist market.'

Stef wasn't about to be put off. 'It's very old,' he said, 'and I thought it might be quite rare. It's a sort of classic, I think.'

Casually – like he'd nothing better to do – the dealer leaned forward, took old Hermann from Stef and had a look inside to check the publication date and stuff. We'd expected him to do that.

Then we studied his expression. He tried dead hard to hide it, but you could tell from the little twitch around his mouth. He'd spotted the signature.

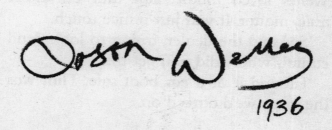

1936

It was written in the top left corner. The ink was really faded. Anna had spent ages getting that bit right. You only had to check her bedroom floor!

'Hmm . . .' murmured the dealer, like it was nothing at all.

Yes!

I mean, he was so obviously suckered. The idea was he'd think Stef was totally clueless about Orson Welles. After all, why should a stupid kid know anything about a legendary film-maker who'd been dead for twenty years?

But the dealer would know. When the dealer was younger, everybody knew about Orson Welles. He was like a cross between Tom Hanks and Steven Spielberg. So his signature in a book was worth something.

The dealer might even know that Orson Welles loved magic. But that bit didn't *really* matter. It was just a nice touch.

'So,' said the dealer, trying to look dead casual, 'where did you get this?'

'I found it at a car boot sale.' That was the story we'd agreed on.

'Stef does magic,' explained Anna, still bright and breezy.

'But I've sort of read it now,' he said. 'And, if I really want, I can always buy a paperback version.' Amazingly, that bit happened to be true.

The dealer rubbed his chin. 'I could give you five pounds for it.'

Five pounds!

I mean, how greedy can you get?

Stef did a brilliant sigh. 'I dunno. I was hoping it was worth a lot more than five pounds.'

The dealer just grinned. 'I don't think so!'

Stef tried to sound dead disappointed. 'It really is a classic magic book.'

'Maybe so,' said the dealer, 'but that doesn't make it valuable.'

That's when Anna chimed in. 'Show him one of the tricks, Stef.' She got the tone just right. Like, somehow, it would help things if he did.

'Yeah, go on, Stef. Show him that card trick.' I felt stupid saying it, but I said it anyway. I thought it might help. It was my contribution.

'Well . . .' said Stef, like, somehow, he could be persuaded. It was a brilliant bit of acting.

The dealer, of course, just looked amused. 'I'm sure your trick is very clever,' he said all patronizing, 'but it's still going to be five pounds.'

'I think I'll leave it then.'

The dealer didn't like that. 'If it would help,' he said, still off-hand, 'I could check it out for you? If you want to leave it with me?'

Well, we weren't having that.

'Thanks,' said Stef reaching out for the book, 'but if it's not valuable, I'd rather just keep it.'

The dealer bit his lip, but he gave Stef the book.

'I like your shop,' said Anna, keeping up the breeziness.

'Have a nice Christmas,' I added, brightly.

And we moved towards the door.

'Listen,' said the dealer with this pathetic chuckle, 'seeing as it *is* Christmas, I'm prepared to make it ten pounds.'

Stef hesitated for ages. 'No . . .' he said at last. 'But thanks anyway.'

Anna pulled on the door.

'Hang on . . .' said the dealer.

We hung on.

Then he said it. 'Um . . . er . . . why don't you show me that trick?'

I felt like punching the air. I bet we all did. Because the greedy dealer was so desperate to keep us in the shop. I mean, how else could he get his hands on the book? How else could he check out the signature? And he could obviously smell a nice fat profit.

In other words, he'd swallowed the hook.

'OK,' said Stef. And he didn't smirk or anything.

Now, next to the armchair was a little table, so Stef gave me the book to hold and we all gathered round. Then Stef took three cards from the pack he had in his pocket.

'Right,' he said. 'This one's called Guard the Lady. The Lady's the Queen of Diamonds, and her bodyguards are these two black twos.'

The dealer could see that.

Then Stef turned the cards over, so the
Queen was in the middle, sort of guarded.

'Now,' he said, 'I'm going to show you
the cards again.'

And he did. He picked them up, showed
off their faces then dropped them back
down. It was pretty clear which one was
the Queen. But just to prove it, Stef picked
up the black twos and showed them off
again.

'Now, do you know where the Queen
is?' he asked the dealer.

Well, of course he did. I mean, it was so
obvious.

'And would you bet on it?'

'Too right I would.' He thought Stef was
joking, didn't he?

'OK,' said Stef. 'Then would you bet . . . that Toby jug I can't afford?'

The dealer seemed to enjoy that idea. 'Against what exactly?'

'Against the book if you like.'

The dealer grinned. 'I just wish you weren't joking,' he said.

'But I'm not,' said Stef, dead calm.

Now, what you have to remember is that the dealer knew where the Queen was. He wasn't stupid. And he'd been keeping a very close watch. I mean, it wasn't even a gamble. He *knew*.

'So,' he said, 'let me get this right. You're telling me that you'll bet your magic book against my Toby jug. And all I have to do is point to the Queen?'

'I'll go better than that,' said Stef. 'If you're wrong I get the jug, but you *still* get the book.'

The dealer thought for a while, then checked that he hadn't misheard.

'That's right,' said Stef. 'Either way, you get the book.'

The greedy dealer must have thought he couldn't lose.

I wish you could have seen his face.
The Queen was a two!

We just had time for a shake. It was touch
and go — Anna had to get to the theatre —
but then we had something big to
celebrate.

'Stef,' said Anna. 'You're a genius!'

Well, he didn't mind hearing that. Up till
then he'd only been fantastic and brilliant.

'Well, you know,' he said, studying his
fingernails.

We knew.

'I still don't get it,' I admitted. 'It was so
obviously the Queen.'

'I do have to have some secrets!'

'It's just a shame you had to lose old
Hermann.'

'Well, we wouldn't have got the jug otherwise. And I *can* always get another copy. It is only a book.'

'I'd love to be there when he finds out Orson Welles wrote his name with a tea bag!'

We all laughed at that. And I'd swear the Toby jug was joining in.

STICKS

Beryl had tears in her eyes.

'Oh Charlie,' she said. 'I don't know what to say. I never thought I'd see him again.'

Beryl gave the jug a big sentimental smile. I knew it meant more to her than she'd admitted.

'Just think of it as a thank you for the drum kit.'

'But it must have cost you all your pocket money!'

If only she knew.

'I had lots of help from Anna and Stef,' I admitted. 'It's sort of from all of us – like a Christmas present.'

'Well, you give them a big thank you from me.'

'I will,' I said. I'd tell them later – at Ellington Moon's party.

Beryl shuffled across to her knick-knack corner and put the jug next to her swan made from shells.

'And there's something else,' I said, remembering. 'Mum says would you like to come round for Christmas dinner?'

Well, she pretended she wasn't sure about that, but I could tell she really wanted to.

'I don't suppose you'll have the time of your life,' I said, 'but Dad's coming along too and, actually, you being there might help keep things . . . you know . . . a bit more relaxed.'

Beryl smiled. 'Then of course I'll come.'

And that was that.

Except, when I got up to leave, she said, 'Will you make me a promise Charlie?'

'Um . . . if I can.' I wondered what was coming next.

'One day,' said Beryl, 'you'll get yourself a new kit.'

I was actually shocked she'd said it. 'Not for ages yet!'

'No, no,' she agreed, 'not for ages of course. But one day . . . you will. And when you do Charlie, promise me you'll try to give my drums to someone like yourself — someone who's keen to learn.'

Well, that was easy. 'All right,' I said. 'I promise.'

But Beryl hadn't finished.

'And whatever you do, never, never, never put the kit in the loft.'

And I never would.

POSTSCRIPT ABOUT THE MAGIC

When I was nine or ten, a very special treat was a trip to London. In those days, of course, there were no McDonalds or multi-screen cinemas or designer label clothes shops. Quite a lot of London was more or less the way Beryl would have remembered when she was drumming in her jazz band. One place she would definitely have known was the Lyons Corner House in Leicester Square. And the best thing about walking through those wonderful doors was the chance to enjoy a huge chocolate and ice cream shake known as a Whipsy.

But, for me, even better than a Whipsy was a trip to Davenport's Magic Shop.

You could find the shop by heading for the British Museum. Davenport's, you see, was right opposite. And you couldn't really miss it anyway, because hanging above the door — a bit like a pub sign — was a rabbit in a top hat.

The shop itself was quite old, Edwardian probably, and, somehow, the look of it felt just right. If you went inside — it told you — you'd be entering a very special world indeed. The big window was full of mysterious decorations, and marvellous-looking tricks, and strange masks.

Now, Davenport's was run by a famous family of magicians, and when you got inside one of them might well be standing behind the long wooden counter. From there they would happily demonstrate all the very latest inventions. And when you bought the trick of your choice it felt like you were becoming a magician yourself.

At the end of the counter and along the opposite wall were big glass cabinets. Inside on display were the special tricks. These

were the props the professionals bought –
Floating Skulls, Chinese Guillotines,
Linking Rings, Disappearing Boxes, Wands
and Canes, Multiplying Candles and Dove
Pans. On one shelf was a happy group of
ventriloquist dummies – all looking like
there was nothing in the world that could
surprise them. And beneath them would be
Mr Punch, surrounded by the characters of
his world.

More than anything, it was the
atmosphere of that shop that got me inter-
ested in magic. And for quite a few years I
did a lot of magic. So when, in the story,
I've described a trick, it really is a proper
trick – something with a logical
explanation.

And can you explain the rope trick?
How did Stef and Anna climb the rope? It's
really not that mysterious. The clues are all
there.

POSTSCRIPT ABOUT THE
DRUMMING

I've never been a drummer but I've played my saxophone alongside a fair few of them. And quite often they've needed Beryl's advice! But the ones who get it right always make the music swing. 'Cos that's the drummer's job.

And if you've ever wondered about drumming yourself, you might try learning to paradiddle. It's not that hard, but then it's not that easy either. So if you can get it right, you've probably got what it takes. Chops!

Now a paradiddle is one of those words that sounds like the thing it's describing. So if you tap an even beat with both hands, going *right left right right left right left left right left right right left right left left*, then you've just tapped out four paradiddles. You could even say the word as you tap the beat.

And if you can't get it right, well at least you'll know. And there are lots of other things you could do — like hunting wild mushrooms, or drawing funny cartoons, or inventing new magic tricks.

ABOUT THE AUTHOR

Whenever he can, Alan Fraser likes to play his saxophone. But at other times he's been an enthusiastic magician, a jug band washboard strummer, a stand-up comedian, a bit of a singer, a composer/bandleader, and the owner of his very own jazz club. There were some other jobs too, but they were all about money – and not much fun at all.

He lives in Oxfordshire and is married with two children.

13 PAIRS OF BLUE SUEDE SHOES
Alan Fraser

What is my dad thinking??

Guess who got the big laugh when
Malcolm Moron told everyone that my
dad sings in a male voice choir?
Me, Sam. And now Dad's planning to
sing AT MY SCHOOL in a
fund-raising concert!

It's even worse for Eddie. His dad is an
Elvis Presley impersonator – and
once he's up on stage doing his act,
Eddie's life might just as well be over.

When Eddie's dad gets together with my
dad and his mates, my life will
be over too...

A hilarious tale of dads in white jumpsuits.
Oh, and don't forget the blue
suede shoes...

CORGI YEARLING BOOKS
0 440 86538 7